SP20000252MAR2011   ISBN: 0-7172-8821-8

Manufactured in the United States of America.
A B C D   1 2 3 4

WALT DISNEY'S
All's Well That Ends Well

GROLIER
BOOK CLUB EDITION

Lady and Tramp have four puppies. Three of the puppies are just like their mother. They are always polite and well-behaved.

The fourth puppy is named Scamp, and he is very much like his father.

Scamp is very curious. He is always
asking questions.

How does a shoe taste?

Why does the garbage smell funny?

What's in the laundry basket?

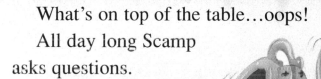

What's on top of the table...oops!
All day long Scamp
asks questions.
Unfortunately,
the answers get him
into a lot of trouble!

Lady is a good mother.
She tries to teach her puppies
good manners.

When Lady walks in the
park, three of her puppies trot
nicely beside her.

But not Scamp! He's
too busy chasing birds!

Scamp wants to be just like his father,
Tramp. But Tramp isn't at all like Lady.
Sometimes Tramp chases big cars.

Sometimes he growls at strange dogs.
Sometimes he even howls at the moon.
Scamp thinks his father is the best-behaved
dog in the world.

Scamp and his family live with Jim Dear
and Darling. They have a small son named Eric.
Scamp wants to be like his father, but when he
howls like Tramp, Darling scolds him.
"No, Scamp," she says. "Polite puppies don't howl!"

Jim Dear and Darling never scold Tramp.
Tramp is their hero! He fetches the newspaper
and finds Eric's lost toys.

Scamp wants to find things, too. Then he will
be a hero, just like his father.

One day Aunt Sara visited. She brought
Eric a present. Darling invited her to see the
puppies. So she put the box on the floor.

Then they went into the kitchen to see Lady
and all her puppies. But Scamp wasn't in the
kitchen. He was hiding under a big chair in the
living room.

Scamp ran up to the big box with the ribbon
on top. He was curious. What could be inside?

In the kitchen, Lady's other
puppies were playing with a little blue ball.
"Aren't they nice?" Eric asked.
Lady looked very proud.

But Aunt Sara wasn't so sure.

"Honestly, I think that puppies are nothing but trouble!" she said with a frown.

"Oh, no!" Darling said, "Lady is such a good mother. Her puppies are no trouble at all."

But when they came back to the living
room, what did they see?

Trouble!

There, next to the open box, sat Scamp.
He was looking at a large, stuffed tiger.

"What did I say?" said Aunt Sara.
"Puppies are nothing but trouble.
He's opened Eric's present. What a
naughty puppy!"

Later, as Aunt Sara was leaving,
she talked about Scamp.

"That puppy is full of mischief,"
she said. "You should give him away."

Scamp was embarrassed. He certainly
had not been a hero.

Later that day, Scamp was playing in the
front garden when he suddenly heard Aunt
Sara's car stop in front of the house.

He watched Aunt Sara walk to the front
door. She looked very sad.

Aunt Sara rang the bell, and Darling opened
the door.

"What's the matter, Aunt Sara?" asked Darling,
seeing her aunt's unhappy face.

"Oh, a terrible thing has happened!" Aunt Sara
answered. "I've lost my little Rose!"

Darling and Aunt Sara went inside, and
Scamp was left staring at the closed door.

Then Scamp had an idea.

This was his big chance to be a hero!

All he had to do was find a little rose for
Aunt Sara. So off he went, in search of a rose.

Scamp trotted off down the street. As
he went, he tried to remember everything
he saw so he wouldn't get lost.

First, he ran beside a wooden fence.
He chased a squirrel up a tree.

Then he jumped into a pile of leaves.
No rose for Aunt Sara in there!

Finally, Scamp came to
a busy street corner.
A deep voice called out,
"Roses! Lovely fresh roses!"

Scamp followed the voice, and suddenly he found himself in front of a store. The store had all kinds of flowers, fruits and vegetables.

Scamp stared
at the lovely
flowers. If only
he could grab a
pretty little rose.

But suddenly the store
owner chased him away.
"Get out of here!" yelled
the man.

Scamp ran away.

He raced around a
corner and into a garden,
where he hid behind
an old wooden fence.

Scamp looked around for the man with the broom. Scamp did not see him, but he did see something else. Something he'd never seen before.

A big tomcat was sleeping
next to a dish of milk.
Scamp had never met a cat.

Scamp was curious. So he walked up to the
cat and gently poked it with his paw. Scamp was
trying to be friendly.

But the tomcat was not friendly.

The cat sprang up and chased poor Scamp.
Scamp had never been so scared in his life!

Scamp ran through a hole in the fence.
He hid bchind a large barrel.
Scamp decided he never
wanted to meet another cat!

Scamp sat and waited until it was safe to come out. Suddenly, he heard a funny little sound. "Meow…meow…"

Scamp looked around. There, in a clump of grass, sat a sweet little kitten.

Oh, no! Not another cat! thought Scamp.

But this cat was tiny and didn't look
dangerous at all.

Scamp was curious. So he decided to take
a closer look.

The little kitten looked sad. Scamp wagged
his tail to cheer it up, but the kitten just kept
on looking sad.

Suddenly, Scamp
remembered the dish
of milk.

Cats must like milk,
he thought. This little
kitten is probably hungry.

So Scamp carefully
crept back into the yard.
Luckily, the big tomcat
was no longer there.

Scamp grabbed
the dish of milk and
ran off!

Scamp carefully carried the dish of milk.
Then he placed the dish in front of the kitten.
Immediately, the kitten lapped up the milk.
She looked very happy.

It was getting late. Scamp decided to look for
Aunt Sara's rose tomorrow. Scamp wanted to go home.
So he sneaked past the owner of the corner store.
He ran beside the wooden fence.

And he jumped into the pile of leaves.
But there was one thing Scamp didn't do.
He did not turn around.

Scamp reached his house and walked up the steps.
Then he heard a funny sound, "Meow…meow."
Scamp turned around. There, behind him, was the
little kitten. It had followed him all the way home!

Scamp did not know
what to do. But before he
could do anything, Darling
opened the front door.

"Aunt Sara, Aunt Sara!"
Darling cried. "Come and
see! Scamp has found your
little Rose!"

That night, the whole family threw a party for Scamp. Darling had baked a cake especially for him.

"Scamp is a real hero!" Aunt Sara said. "He found my little Rose when I thought I had lost her forever."

Lady and Tramp looked proudly at Scamp. Little Rose purred happily in Aunt Sara's arms.

Scamp wondered why Aunt Sara called her cat a rose, but he would ask his parents later.

Right now, there was something he was more curious about.

How does cake taste?